Your path is made for a journey, not a destination.

WRITTEN & ILLUSTRATED BY
PETER SIMPSON COOK

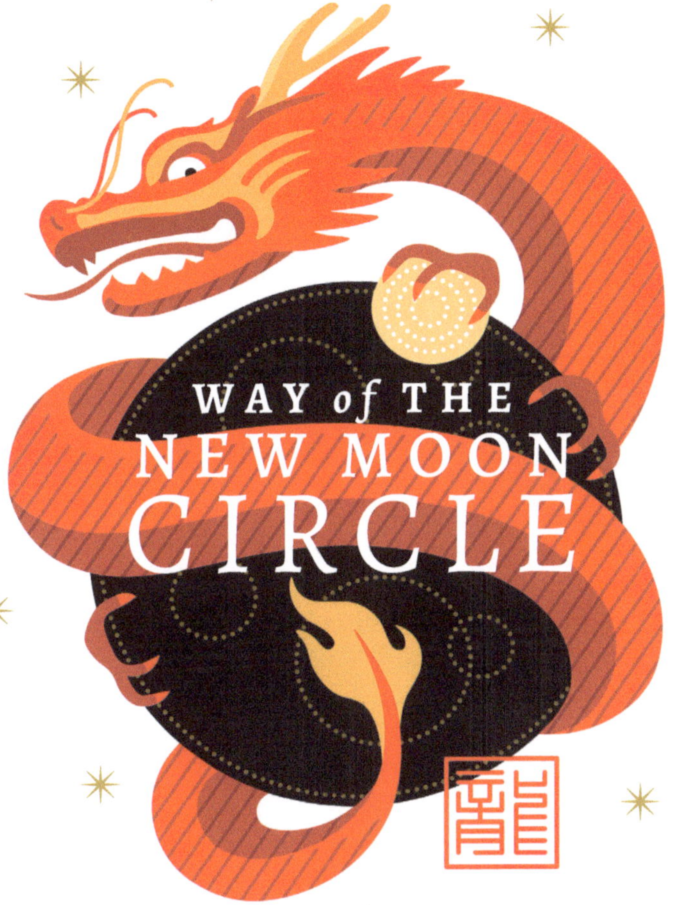

QUAIL BOOKS | PSC PUBLISHING

WAY OF THE NEW MOON CIRCLE
Written & Illustrated by Peter Simpson Cook
studiopsc@gmail.com

A short full-color illustrated novel—for readers of all ages.

Library of Congress Control Number: 2025902149
ISBN 979-8-9925459-0-6 (Paperback Full-Color Illustrated Edition)
ISBN 979-8-9925459-1-3 (Hardcover Full-Color Illustrated Edition)

Front cover quote by LAO TZU.

ACKNOWLEDGMENTS
Thank you for your creative insights, expert knowledge and support:
Susan M. Blake, Christine Cava Preston, Kathleen Riley, Sean Riley & May Sun.

Designed by Peter Simpson Cook
Produced by PSC Art Studio for Quail Books and PSC Publishing
California, United States of America.

pscpublishing.com

CONTENTS

THE EMPEROR'S RACE: A Prologue by the Cat, pages 6-9

1- THE RAT of the Blossoming Plum Tree, pages 12-15

2- THE OX of the Distant Meadow, pages 16-19

3- THE TIGER of the Deep Deep Jungle, pages 20-23

4- THE RABBIT of Whatever Comes Next, pages 24-27

5- THE DRAGON of the Tall Smoky Mountain, pages 28-31

6- THE SNAKE of the Sheltering Stones Spa, pages 32-35

7- THE HORSE of the Boundless Plain, pages 36-39

8- THE SHEEP of the Misty Rolling Hills, pages 40-43

9- THE MONKEY of the Shadowland Lagoon, pages 44-47

10- THE ROOSTER of the Sundial Pagoda, pages 48-51

11- THE DOG of the Resplendent Village, pages 52-55

12- THE BOAR of the Stately Grove, pages 56-59

12 ½- THE WAY of the New Moon Circle, pages 60-63

13- THE FORTUNE CAT of the Moon Gate Garden, pages 64-69

14- AN EPILOGUE: The New Year Panda, pages 70-75

15- AFTERWORD: The Circle of Animals, pages 79-97
  Years of the RAT, page 80 / Years of the OX, page 81
  Years of the TIGER, page 82 / Years of the RABBIT, page 83
  Years of the DRAGON, page 84 / Years of the SNAKE, page 85
  Years of the HORSE, page 86 / Years of the SHEEP, page 87
  Years of the MONKEY, page 88 / Years of the ROOSTER, page 89
  Years of the DOG, page 90 / Years of the BOAR, page 91
  The CAT, page 92 / The PANDA, page 93
  QUOTES, listings and credits, pages 94, 95
  AUTHOR'S NOTE, page 96

THE EMPEROR'S RACE

A PROLOGUE BY THE CAT

This is a foreward-*ish*/introduction-*ish*/preface-*ish* kind of thing that I was "asked" to compose to bring readers, like yourself, up to speed on the back story of all this zodiac animal business. Since I didn't make the cut for the top twelve animal slots, I thought, why not? I can write a prologue and my "unique perspective" is as good as the next animal's, right? (Come to think of it, I was the next animal—number thirteen.) Anyway, my point is that I have an exclusive frame of reference for telling this story about the Emperor's Race, and that could prove to be very interesting because of who I am—the cat.

Why a particular order for these zodiac animals in the first place? The answer is found in an ancient Chinese legend about a Great Race that was organized to determine in what progression the competing animals crossed the finish line. The multiple versions of this myth all begin with the Jade Emperor (ruler of heaven and earth, by the way) deciding it would be easier for his people to measure time if he gave them a proper calendar. He decided to name each year after one of twelve animals calling it a zodiac and declared a race between all the animals to determine the order of the twelve years. The details of the race vary in many versions of the legend, but most start the race on land and reach a climax crossing a river to the finish line at the Emperor's palace.

This is where I come in. All versions of the race focus primarily on the winner—the rat. The ox and myself are supporting characters as the rat beats us both. Some narratives record how I may have "napped" through the race or that the rat "forgot" to register me before the start of the competition (since we were "pals" at this point in our lives). Other story lines describe how the rat pushes me into the river from the ox's back, thus eliminating me completely from making the top twelve. As rats and cats are swimming challenged, the rat somehow convinces the ox to give us a lift across the river by singing or sweet talking. Then, as the ox reaches the other side, the rat pushes me into the river, jumps onto the river bank ahead of the ox and finishes the race coming in first, the ox second, and I wind up treading water or drowning (which obviously didn't happen because here I am to tell the tale).

The variety of renditions at the beginning of this myth beg the question: If I'm not part of the zodiac exclusive club of animals, why give me all the precious story telling time at the top of this fable? I'll tell you why—because people LOVE CATS! I'm popular, and my obvious absence from this calendar needs an explanation. I believe there's something fishy about my total exclusion from the circle. So, Voilà! Mistakes were made! (Here's that "unique perspective" I was telling you about). Mark my words, there's more to this story. But, I digress. On with the race!

Next up are the tiger, rabbit and dragon stories which are pretty much the same in most versions. The tiger is a very capable contender and while swimming across the river was delayed by a strong current and comes in third. In the wake of the tiger's crossing, sails the rabbit who hops on the river's stepping stones and then onto a floating log that drifts off course. The flying mythical dragon blows the rabbit forward to the river's bank and thus sacrifices that fourth spot to the rabbit. The dragon, (who you would think would win the race because DRAGONS CAN FLY) was late to the party bringing rain to parched farms and villages, saving them from famine—but even so, came in fifth.

The story continues with the galloping and swimming horse giving a joyride to an unknown commuter—the snake! As you can imagine, the snake (which was wrapped around the front leg of the horrified horse) uncoiled and flung itself just in time to come in sixth, and the horse seventh.

By now, the narrative seems to lose interest in the details of the remaining five animals. Most versions recount how the sheep, monkey and rooster, working together as a team, found a raft and sailed across the river. They didn't seem to care about what order they reached the finish line, as the sheep secured the eighth spot, the monkey the ninth and the rooster rounded out the top ten.

This lack of urgency continued as the dog seemed to have been distracted by having fun, running in circles and basically living in the moment, enjoying the day by the river and coming in eleventh. While, you guessed it, the boar feasted and slept (like pigs do) and couldn't be bothered rushing to the finish line—coming in last.

After the conclusion of the race when the rat didn't apologize to me, I decided to let go of the past. You may now understand why I have a strained relationship with the rat. As the years have rolled by we seem to just avoid each other. You see, I'm not a vengeful cat, but a curious creature and a serene feline that prefers to go with the flow. It may surprise you to know that I like to observe the souls of this world and be of assistance if needed because of my belief in karma and what goes around does come around. Rant over.

On these pages begins a different tale for the twelve animals as the cycle of the new moon moves closer to the twelfth lunar year. Even now, the wheels are in motion for an unpredicted journey down an unexpected path (with a few surprises of my own). I've waited for over eleven long boring years since the Emperor's Race—what's a few more days?

- THE CAT

9

Then, with the nonchalance of an experienced guide, the feline stood, yawned, stretched and wandered out through the moon gate...

WAY *of* THE NEW MOON CIRCLE

YEARS OF THE RAT
With auspicious rat characteristics and other significant insights on page 80.

- 1 -

THE RAT

OF THE BLOSSOMING PLUM TREE

It was a night for either *staying* or *going*. But the rat, sitting alone in the Blossoming Plum Tree, didn't know that yet.

Even though the moon's bright light was creeping across the arched gate and spring's first blossom petals were drifting to the ground, the complacent rat was oblivious to all this movement and was content to remain in the plum tree, thus avoiding the flow of life.

However, tonight an invitation had arrived and the rat was worried that it would change everything.

Jumping from the tree, the distressed rat paced across the top of the moon gate. "Oh dear, oh dear, oh dear! This feeling of uncertainty has got me all in a dither," thought the fretting rat silhouetted by the already waning moon. "Being the first animal is a huge responsibility and where on earth is this *New Moon Circle?*"

It had been twelve years since the Jade Emperor's race to determine the order of the twelve zodiac animals. The invitation stated that in twelve days and on this month's new moon, the animals were to gather for a reunion at a secret location.

The enveloped card clearly requested that it was the responsibility of each animal to rely on their inner strengths to discover the circle's location. The animals must arrive at the New Moon Circle in the same order they crossed the finish line at the Emperor's race twelve years earlier. Except, the rat had taken quick advantage to win the race.

"Where could this *circle* possibly be," questioned the desperate rat pacing over the arch, "and how could someone so pocket-sized as myself have such an enormous task?" Even the rat's tiny shadow cast by the luminous moon seemed to illustrate the point.

Stopping at the exact center on top of the moon gate, the thinking rat's mind cleared, as an ancient proverb by an old master seemed to whisper to the rat's soul. *A journey of a thousand miles begins with a single step.*

"Perhaps, my *single step* is asking for help," reasoned the rat. "The ox is the second animal and may know the location of the circle. As much as I want to avoid the ox, I must humble myself and respectfully apologize for my behavior at the race twelve years ago."

Feeling resolute, the rat shouted out, "I will begin by searching for the ox!—Oh, I must calm myself," said the alert rat, hearing a purring sound coming from below.

Looking down, the rat saw a black cat walking slowly under the gate splashing and distorting the moon's reflection on a puddle of water. Without a sound, the creeping rat inched down through the branches of the plum tree to get a better look.

With heart pounding and taking a deep breath, the timid rat asked, "Excuse me, my feline friend. I'm the rat of the Blossoming Plum Tree and I'm looking for an ox. Have you seen an ox?"

The hungry cat looked up and with a half smile replied, "We used to be friends you and I, but now—not so much. Tell you what, rat, yesterday I heard about an ox tying Chinese knots in the Distant Meadow. If you let me come with you, I will take you to that ox."

"To be honest, I would rather you just give me directions to the ox," said the reluctant, but shrewd rat. "However, if you insist on joining me, you must promise to honor our old friendship and not make me your supper tonight. Agreed?"

"Agreed," purred the cat licking its paw.

Then, with the nonchalance of an experienced guide, the feline stood, yawned, stretched and wandered out through the moon gate along an ancient stone passage.

"Wait! I'll follow you," shouted the resolved rat leaping from the plum tree that let go of the most resilient blossom petals which fell onto the cat's meandering path.

"Do try to keep up—if you can," mumbled the aloof cat without turning, while the rat trailed behind.

And so, under the waning moon and leaving the Blossoming Plum Tree behind them, the rat and the cat began their journey through the moon gate to find the ox that was tying Chinese knots in the Distant Meadow.

YEARS OF THE OX
With auspicious ox characteristics and other significant insights on page 81.

- 2 -

THE OX

OF THE DISTANT MEADOW

"Oh, look what a mess I have made," said the discouraged ox standing motionless in the Distant Meadow after another unsuccessful morning trying to tie Chinese knots. Covered in red string, the large ox's horns, hooves and tail were enveloped by looping cords, like a bowl of slippery noodles.

"I set out to try something new yesterday, but it's obvious, my big strong body is not built for the delicate task of knot tying." The stubborn ox's patience was wearing thin and with a loud sigh it exhaled, "I don't like to give up a challenge so soon. But, what can I do?"

After walking all night the rat and the cat were warming themselves in the sun near a fence. Not far away, they overheard the ox bellowing its frustrations.

"Let me do the talking," said the rat as they crept along the long dusty road and into the tall grass of the meadow. A gentle breeze fluttered the varieties of red cord, ribbon and string that were strewn across the ox's fenced paddock like abandoned streamers from yesterday's parade.

"Remember *me*, old friend?" greeted the hesitant rat cautiously approaching the snorting ox. "I wanted to say how sorry I am that we got off on the wrong foot—or rather hoof. But, I—it seemed like the astute thing to do when I—er, jumped from your back after you swam me to shore. How was I to know that the Jade Emperor would make me the first zodiac animal and you the second? I say we let bygones be bygones—all right? Old chap?"

"Was *that* an apology, rat? I'm not sure, but it sounded *something* like an apology," sighed the exhausted ox and then continued through gritted teeth. "But, I'm desperate—so, if you can assist me out of this web of string, I will relent and forgiveness is yours."

"That, I can manage. However, this cat and I will help untangle you and tie your knot, on one condition: that you help us find the New Moon Circle before the Lunar New Year," proposed the cunning rat.

"I could use the excuse that I'm all tied up and can't help you," snorted the humorless ox, "but I don't think knot tying is something I will get better at with practice. I realize I'm not built for it. However, anything that requires brute strength—well, I'm the one for the job!"

"It's great to try new things—I get it," interjected the casual cat looking on. "But, you must also know your limitations, my pal. So, do we hear a 'yes'?"

"Well, I've never heard of this *New Moon Circle* and if I did, I don't think it's around here," said the ox. "The tiger of the Deep Deep Jungle, with whom I've kept in touch since the race twelve years ago, is likely to know were this circle may be."

"If you give us a ride to find the tiger and join us on our quest, we promise to restore your dignity and free you from these binding red cords," reasoned the rat. "Do we have an arrangement?"

"This sounds like a grand adventure and to tell you the truth, I have become set in my ways as of late. So, YES, we are in agreement," shouted the trustworthy ox.

Working their small bodies and fingers, the rat and cat set the ox free and obsessively wound all the cords, ribbons and string into a gigantic red ball. Then, using a length of the red cord they tied an exquisite Pan Chang knot that looked as if it could go on forever with no beginning or end.

"Ahhhhhh," sighed the ox, calming down by taking in a series of full breaths and then releasing them with a blast through both nostrils. "That's better—I'm feeling grounded, centered and empowered again!" said the ox and then promptly headed for the open gate.

So, together the rat and the cat (sitting on the ox with the Pan Chang knot hanging from its neck) left the Distant Meadow and headed down the long dusty road for the Deep Deep Jungle.

YEARS OF THE TIGER
With auspicious tiger characteristics and other significant insights on page 82.

- 3 -
THE TIGER
OF THE DEEP DEEP JUNGLE

"We let the tiger come to us," said the cat jumping down from the ox's back, as the sound of a distant gong echoed through the trees stopping the rat and the ox dead in their tracks.

"Bengal tigers are my cousins, so I know what I'm talking about," continued the cat. "Besides, this tiger's been tracking us for hours. I say, let's stop here, take a nap and see whatever comes next."

The afternoon sunlight was streaming through the lush green bamboo and vines making the path before them visible in the darkening jungle. Stillness crept around them as the gong sound faded to silence. But, a nap was soon out of the question as the Deep Deep Jungle abruptly became alive with the calls of exotic birds, screams of animals and the beating of tanggu drums that swelled like a strong heartbeat into a loud frenzy.

Suddenly, with a thundering GONG, a majestic tiger appeared on the trail before them. The tiger's sharp teeth held tight the wooden stick of a long mallet and its tail was wrapped around a brass gong.

"Halt! I am the 'Commander of Crescendo' and the 'Sovereign of Sound,'" roared the bold tiger setting down the gong and mallet.

"To gain entrance to this jungle you must be announced with this royal gong," decreed the boastful tiger, "or I, as the 'Prefect of Percussion' and 'Magistrate of Music', will devour you all at my next feast!"

"Not so fast, 'Ruler of Racket,'" snapped the cat coming forward. "As your urban relation, I simply ask you to let us pass through your stomping grounds, answer a few questions and we'll be on our way."

"Your majesty," interrupted the ox appealing to the tiger's vanity, "'tis I, your colleague, the ox. Since you are the third animal in the zodiac order after me, we're hoping that with your imperial wisdom, you can direct us to the New Moon Circle before the Lunar New Year?"

The pompous tiger considered the question and then replied. "Well, since you put it that way, I'll let you thrive another day, old friend!"

At which the tiger's teeth picked up the mallet and began a series of deafening GONGS that went on for entirely too long. Then, the good humored tiger boomed two or three more GONGS announcing each animal of the traveling party.

"You had me there for a minute, tiger," laughed the ox.

"It's great to see you again, my good ox. However, what are you doing with the rat and cat riding on your back, yet again?" continued the tiger who was skilled at speaking out the side of its mouth while biting the mallet. "Don't you remember their deception at the race?"

"All is forgiven. We are friends now because we are on a most incredible adventure. You see, we need your talents and wise expertise to guide us to the New Moon Circle by the Lunar New Year!"

"This circle has not been made known to me yet," whispered the tiger with shallow humility. "I have a feeling that this could be another competition. So, if you permit me to bravely lead you on this noble quest, with the advantages of my dazzling hearing and extraordinary eyesight, I'll discover this circle forthwith."

"Let's stop here tonight then" interjected the practical rat, speaking up. "Tomorrow we'll let you guide us, on three conditions: "firstly—keep the gong playing to a minimum; secondly—remember this is a quest, *not* a competition; and thirdly—please don't eat us!"

"Agreed," grinned the charming tiger.

With that all settled, the animals bedded down, but to their annoyance the jungle sounds kept them tossing and turning all night.

Up early the next morning, the imperious tiger announced the start of their quest with the usual fanfare of a small ceremony including an inspiring speech and (of course) the sound of the royal GONG-G-G-G-G.

Then, yawning and still sleepy, the rat, the cat, and the ox were conducted through the Deep Deep Jungle by the tiger (aka: the 'Baron of Bongs') to find the New Moon Circle or whatever would come next.

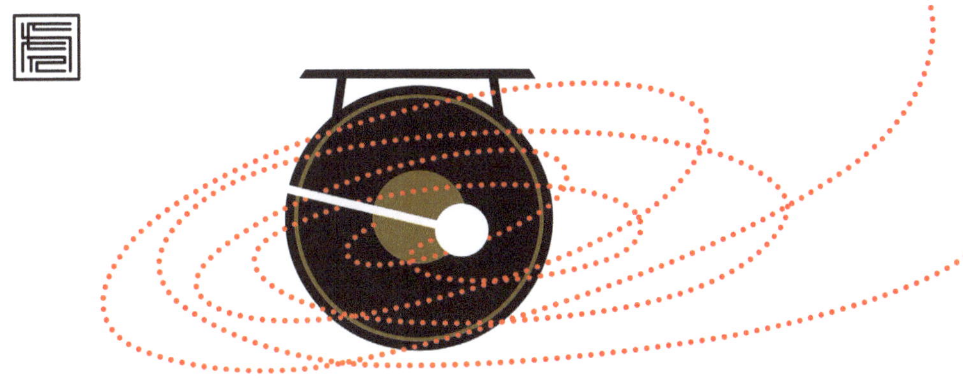

YEARS OF THE RABBIT
With auspicious rabbit characteristics and other significant insights on page 83.

- 4 -

THE RABBIT

OF WHATEVER COMES NEXT

"I don't see any sign of the circle, only miles of scrub-land covered in silver grass and reeds," complained the weary rat.

Spreading before the four travelers, the brightest stars were just appearing as the fading colors of a golden sunset kissed the top of the grasslands. Since dawn, the grandiose tiger had been their guide out of the humid shadowy jungle, and then through endless territories like The Middle Of Nowhere, Wide Open Spaces, As Far As You Can See and eventually Over The Hill. Now they stood exhausted and ready to flop.

The sleepy ox yawned, "Are we going... in the right... direc...tion?"

"I do believe we have arrived at Whatever Comes Next," stated the tiger with a few GONGS! "Which reminds me of the old proverb: *If you do not change direction, you may end up where you are heading.*"

"I really don't see... how that helps..." continued the yawning ox, "and besides, with you it's always... 'gong this' and 'gong...,'" but was too tired to argue and collapsed into immediate slumber using the grass as a soft bed.

Being nocturnal, the tiger and cat decided to explore the night sky by tracking the path of the waning moon hoping it would lead them to the New Moon Circle. The darkening sky of the meadowland made it possible to see the Milky Way Galaxy and the stars of many constellations in a great canopy above them.

"To a mind that is still, the whole universe surrenders," whispered the now quiet tiger remembering another proverb by an old wise scholar.

Feeling fatigued, as the light of dawn stretched its first subtle rays on the horizon, they returned to sleep with the group.

The loud snoring of the dozing ox shattered the stillness of the quiet morning, as a cautious and curious rabbit bounced from its cozy burrow to discover who was making all the racket.

"What's that you're carrying, rabbit?" asked the rat while climbing over the sleeping ox. "A red packet of coins, perhaps?"

"Oh m-my" stuttered the surprised rabbit. "If you're h-here to rob me, go ahead and take all these coins, for I can always get more. You see, I really d-don't care about money and I never seem to run out. The r-red packets are for gift giving and bring luck. Wait—excuse me, do I *know* you?" asked the inquisitive rabbit hopping about. "You came here for the moon viewing festival! No? Oh, I know—you're the rat who came in first, and I, fourth, at the Emperor's race! I say, I could b-beat you if we raced again."

"We don't have time for a race right now because we're on a quest," yawned the stretching rat. "The ox, tiger, cat, and myself are all working together to find the New Moon Circle. We must find it by the Lunar New Year in the next few days. Will you help us?"

"Of course I will," replied the thinking rabbit. "You know, there's a powerful D-Dragon in the T-Tall Smoky Mountain that flies over these fields and may have seen this circle you speak of."

"Good thinking generous rabbit!" exclaimed the waking tiger with a hearty GONG while eavesdropping on their conversation. "Last night, after reading the stars, the cat and I discovered that our best course is straight to the Dragon's mountain. That magical and enchanting creature must know where this circle is."

Then, pulling the rabbit aside, the tiger shamelessly hinted, "I've heard how this Dragon *loves* riches... and... I see you have many gold coins... in that crimson packet...? *For G-I-V-I-N-G...?*"

"What the 'Leader of Loud' is trying to say is," interrupted the cat rolling its eyes, "you can hang with us if you give the dragon all your yuan in exchange for Intel about the N.M.C. Agreed?"

"A-a-agreed," stammered the startled and hesitant rabbit.

And with that, the rabbit (with the red packet of coins) joined the rat, cat, ox, and tiger, and left Whatever Comes Next by hopping down the path of the waning moon toward the Tall Smoky Mountain.

YEARS OF THE DRAGON
With auspicious dragon characteristics and other significant insights on page 84.

- 5 -

THE DRAGON

OF THE TALL SMOKY MOUNTAIN

The long climb to the summit of the Tall Smoky Mountain left the group of four animals gasping for breath in the thin air. Before them was a massive stone arch and the entrance to the dragon's lair. A constant thin trail of smoke escaped from the top of the cave continuing up into the pale sky giving the mountain the appearance of a dying volcano.

"I believe I hear crying and the sound of a very large nose being blown," said the tiger looking into the shadowy cavern. "Rabbit, you go in first and see what's afoot."

The dragon's blackened cave was piled high with gold coins, fireworks, scorched furniture and framed photographs of dear departed dragons of days gone by. Vaguely visible through the choking vapor and among these mounds, was the sorrowful dragon's enormous head resting near a glowing brass vessel. Smoldering incense filled the cauldron sending smoke curling around the weepy dragon's sharp teeth and then passed through one flared nostril and out the other with each hopeless breath.

Peering into the smoke-filled stone cavity, the shaking rabbit stood alone at the entrance and stammered bravely, "L-Lord D-Dragon, I am the r-rabbit that you h-helped at the Emperor's r-race and I am here to f-fulfill my k-karmic debt. I've maneuvered up this tall smoky mountain following the w-waning moon to give you this p-packet of gold coins. Also, I was hoping to ask for your urgent help with another matter, but... Hello? Pardon... Can you hear me?"

"Give it a rest!" muttered the blubbering dragon. "What do I care anymore. I'm miserable, can't you see? I'm no use to you because I exchanged my power for hording material possessions and self pity. Now I've been brought to earth as punishment and all I can do is breathe fire, but I 'can't bring rain,'" air quoted the sarcastic dragon with its sharp talons. "Leave me in peace. Now go! And take that adorable fluffy white tail with you!"

"My mistake. You see, I was looking for a NOBLE dragon," said the brave rabbit stepping forward, "an HONORABLE dragon that symbolizes power, luck and success—a dragon that is a supernatural being that can fly without wings! Can you help me find THAT dragon? If not, I'll take my gold coins and go."

"Hold on," replied the blinking and sniffling dragon. "No need to be so hasty, my little friend. Tell me, what's this all about?"

Suddenly calm, the rabbit found a new voice.

"Please do try to pull yourself together, dragon," exclaimed the rabbit. "We're all at our wit's end looking for the New Moon Circle without much success. In six days the animals of the Great Race have been invited to a Lunar New Year reunion at an unknown and mysterious orbicular location. The rat, ox, tiger, and cat, who are my traveling companions, and stand outside this very cave, wondered if you have seen this circle whilst flying over the countryside? Perhaps?"

Impressed by the rabbit's sudden transformation, the dragon's mind whirled with new possibilities and shook off the coating of ash that had settled on its scaled body.

"I have a fantastic idea," shouted the excited dragon standing up. "Oh, I love challenges and crave excitement! Let's you and I fly until we find this *circle* before the others do! We'd make a good team, you and I, with my competitive edge and your no-nonsense diplomacy and navigation skills—together, we'll go further."

With great pomp the dragon rose up and thundered, "Do you, rabbit (who came in forth at the Emperor's race and beat me) agree to join me in this quest?"

"A-a-agreed," stammered the hesitant, rather shocked rabbit.

And with that, the rabbit hopped upon the dragon's back and together they flew out of the cave and disappeared into the floating fluffy white clouds.

YEARS OF THE SNAKE
With auspicious snake characteristics and other significant insights on page 85.

- 6 -

THE SNAKE

OF THE SHELTERING STONES SPA

The waiting rat, cat, ox, and tiger stood gasping outside the cave when the dragon (with the rabbit riding on its back) burst through the lair's entrance and flew skyward shouting down to them, "We'll find the circle first!"

The rat weakly sighed, "it's not a competition..." and in that moment noticed the dragon's neglected letter box was stuffed with what seemed to be junk mail.

"RELAX AND INDULGE YOURSELF AT THE SNAKE'S SHELTERING STONES SPA—Located in the Desert Oasis below the Tall Smoky Mountain," read the rat to the others from an advertising brochure.

"I could use a hot bath," said the ox. "And I, a massage," exclaimed the tiger. "Sign me up for a mani-pedi," added the cat. "Yes, maybe a little acupuncture would be nice," said the rat.

Without further discussion, the travelers set off for the Sheltering Stones Spa. As their self-appointed leader, the tiger directed them down a long trail that seemed to serpentine its way over a mesa, twisting and turning down a canyon and slinking through a vast expanse of arid land.

As dusk arrived, the moon appeared on the dark horizon like a yin-yang symbol being equal parts light and shadow. Moving on, the four travelers slid down rocky slopes and stumbled over large boulders onto the hot flat desert floor. For shelter, they gathered under an ancient tree whose gnarled branches supported various sized gourds hanging from lashings, knots, and braided ropes.

"Listen," said the dust covered ox, "...it's the sound of silence."

A deep weariness seemed to envelop the animals and they dared not move for fear of breaking some kind of unwritten law of nature. Like standing in a dizzying mirage, they looked around and found themselves surrounded by a large group of twelve sandstone monoliths that were arranged in a feng shui aesthetic circle with the timeworn tree at its center.

"I have done it! I have led us to the New Moon Circle," shouted the boastful tiger and punctuated it with a loud echoing GONG!

"Ssssilence," hissed a snake wrapped around a hanging gourd above them. "Ssssurrender," whispered the mysterious golden snake after a pause.

In a trance, the four animals looked up as if under a spell and followed the snake's rational directions without one word of dissent—even the tiger did exactly as instructed dropping the gong and mallet.

"Ssssit," continued the snake looking down at four grass mats in the sand. "Ssssip," said the calm snake pouring fresh water from the Wulu gourd. "Ssssoak," instructed the snake leading them to a cool spring in the shadow of a mammoth rock. "Ssssleep," smiled the tranquil snake providing comfortable pillows and pads.

"Once unstable—now balanced," breathed the ox, as the animals sat, drank, bathed, and zonked out.

In the morning as the others slept, the ox felt a connection to the harmonious energy of the area. Wandering through the massive stones, the ox thought that this *must* be the circle they have been searching for.

"This place is perfect, quiet, calm, and sssssstill," chuckled the ox.

Listening, the undetected snake secretly slithered around the rippling spring to hear the ox's words more clearly.

"I wish we could stay here until the Lunar New Year. Would the snake agree to such an idea, I wonder?" questioned the ox, looking down at the pool's reflection of its hanging red Pan Chang knot.

"Sssscertainly," agreed the snake silently whispering in the shadows, disappearing under a sheltering stone.

Then in that moment, a gentle sultry breeze kicked up from the desert that knocked the hanging gourds like hollow chimes, as the dragon's shadow briefly darkened the oasis below, and then flew on.

YEARS OF THE HORSE
With auspicious horse characteristics and other significant insights on page 86.

- 7 -

THE HORSE

OF THE BOUNDLESS PLAIN

A crack of lightening lit up the morning desert sky followed by a long rolling sound of thunder that echoed off the huge sandstone rocks of the circle. The waking animals gathered for safety around the old tree as a gust of humid air encompassed the amphitheater and whispered a warning—*something is coming.*

In a cyclonic fashion, the golden horse of the Boundless Plain arrived faster than the wind and raced around the tree at the center of the spa's aesthetic arena of monoliths. The magnificent steed came to a sudden halt before the coiled snake among the tree's roots.

"Greetings, Six," panted the gallant horse in a respectful tone.

"Sssseven," responded the serene snake.

"I see you have company," stated the sweating stallion looking at the travelers while fanning off with a red kite-like fan that was tied to its tail. "As I crossed the boundless plain for my cupping appointment today," the chatty horse continued, "I heard on the breeze that the dragon has taken flight again. Do you know why, wise snake?"

"Ssssearching," stated the agile snake.

"We haven't seen the dragon in years. What on earth could that mythical beast be looking for?" asked the horse. "I wonder…"

"Pardon me, that would be the New Moon Circle," explained the timid rat, joining the snake in the shade. "You see, we're all at sixes and sevens wondering where the secret location of this circle may be. For in a few days, we, the Emperor's race winners, have been requested to attend a reunion there on the Lunar New Year."

"But, now that the New Moon Circle is here," interrupted the tiger, "surely our search is over and we can enjoy the spa like royalty."

"What? You must be joking! This is not *the circle*," said the arrogant horse. "My ally, this intuitive snake, just told me that the great dragon is currently at flight over these lands and is seeking it still."

"Whoa! Hold yourself, strong stallion," interjected the cat. "Aren't you and the snake enemies since the Emperor's race? Didn't this sly snake scare you and then cross the finish line before you?"

"Once foes—now friends. This discreet snake treats me here at the spa for my tired legs," explained the horse. "This circle must be beyond the Boundless Plain in the cultural land of the Misty Rolling Hills. I'll race there and discover it FIRST before the dragon does!"

"Excuse me, again," interrupted the brave rat looking up at the horse. "Not to spoil your moment, but it's NOT A COMPETITION!" Trembling, the rat continued, "The invitation clearly states that we must use our individual strengths and arrive all together as a group."

After a long pause, the ox whispered, "Once a race—now a quest."

Corrected, the humbled horse bowed to the others and spoke, "Forgive my over-confident nature. I now see that our efforts must be united and in balance." Then rising upon hind legs the persuasive horse shouted, "The roar of a gale is calling us all to action! Together, we can find the circle in time. Who will join me in this noble quest?"

"We will!" Shouted the tiger, rat, and cat together roused by the horses inspiring speech—but the ox closed its eyes and said nothing.

Desiring to rest at the spa, the silent ox looked at an inscription cut into one of the sheltering stones and read the words of a wise old master: "*With no desire, at rest and still, All things go right as of their will.*"

"Sssstay," said the sympathetic snake to the ox.

The insightful horse saw the look in the snake's eyes and knew what must be done. Then turning to the loyal ox said, "I'm afraid the snake would not make the long journey and needs a friend here, good ox. We will return for you both on the eve of the Lunar New Year and bring you to the New Moon Circle when it is found. Agreed?"

"Yessssss," smiled the snake and the agreeable ox together.

Large drops of rain began to pelt the spa. It was time to race the darkening storm through the desert.

Over the knocking echo of bamboo wind chimes they shouted their good-byes as the rat and cat climbed onto the horse's back. Then with the tiger at their side, together they sped across the Boundless Plain, like a kite cut loose on the wind to the Misty Rolling Hills.

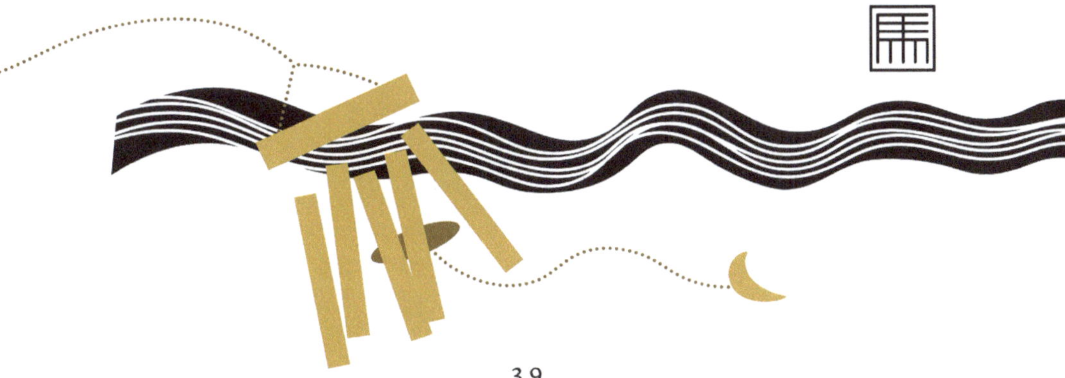

YEARS OF THE SHEEP
With auspicious sheep characteristics and other significant insights on page 87.

- 8 -

THE SHEEP
OF THE MISTY ROLLING HILLS

"It's completely socked in," groaned the travelers in unison. A moist fog blanketed the Misty Rolling Hills which brought the exhausted rat, cat, tiger, and horse to an abrupt stop, unable to move–one–step–further.

The four animals were perspiring from their marathon run at full speed across the Boundless Plain. The wind gusts had whipped the horse's tail releasing the fan to drift away like a kite, while the rat and the cat had held onto the horse's mane like jockeys to the finish line.

"Wait—do you hear something like the clanging of a bell?" asked the alert tiger using its fine tuned hearing.

"That, my friends, is the sound of a sheep," declared the horse. "We will follow the bell's tinkling sound and discover the sheep-cote!"

As the exhausted animals slowly climbed to their feet, the fog lifted and the sunset broke through perfectly placed clouds. The hills beyond were dotted with endless flocks of white and black sheep with bells clanging in all directions. Nonplussed, the animals stared everywhere at once as the impulse to spend the night counting sheep was too overwhelming and fell asleep exactly where they stood.

At daybreak, the bewildered animals awoke near a calm and mighty ram who was wearing a clanging bell around its neck and a carved calligrapher's ink brush in its mouth. Behind the ram on the sheep-cote's walls, hung many crimson banners, scrolls, and couplets with carefully painted black Chinese characters drying in the breeze. On the hillside were flocks of ewes, lambs, and goats receiving silent instruction in the fine art of calligraphy from the ram.

"We don't mean to disturb you," interrupted the hesitant rat as the refreshed travelers inched closer to the master calligrapher, "but, firstly—would you happen to know if the New Moon Circle is hidden among these green and grassy dales, glens, and valleys? If not, then secondly—could you tell us where it might be? We are willing to pay, if, thirdly—you could perhaps lead us there—please?"

Without a word, the ram handed a tasseled scroll for the rat to read and then patiently returned to a silent practice of brushwork.

"I've been expecting you," read the astonished rat unrolling the scroll of the sheep's previously crafted words. *"For it is written that when the cycle of the moon is on the fourth day before the new moon, a dragon with a hare on its back will fly over the misty rolling hills and disappear into the west. Within a day, a group of unlikely traveling companions will come out of the fog, fall asleep and then ask three annoying questions. The answers to these questions are as follows: 1. No. 2. Yes. 3. Maybe."*

"Will I help you? Perhaps, but let me put it in words that you will understand," continued the rat reading the voiceless ram's words. *"I will do as you ask on two conditions: firstly—you all remember that your path is made for a journey, not a destination. And secondly—that you help our flock transport these banners, scrolls, and couplets to the marketplace of the Resplendent Village for the coming new year celebration. Only then will I take you to see someone very special who will know where to find the New Moon Circle. Are we in agreement?"*

Astounded, the rat, cat, tiger, and horse all nodded 'yes.' Then, the ram presented a second scroll for the cat to read, *"Sign here... and initial here... and here... and, finally... here."*

After the rat signed where instructed, the flock quietly loaded a cart half filled with rolled banners, scrolls, and couplets that were written with characters for luck, good fortune, peace, and protection.

With what seemed like no will of their own, the travelers bridled the horse for the trip and in the cart, the cat sat beside the rat holding the reigns. Astonishingly and with complete obedience, the tiger quietly followed biting the mallet and dragging the gong with its tail.

Within minutes they found themselves contently following the speechless ram (with the clanging bell) and were caravaning down the long road through the Misty Rolling Hills to the marketplace of the Resplendent Village.

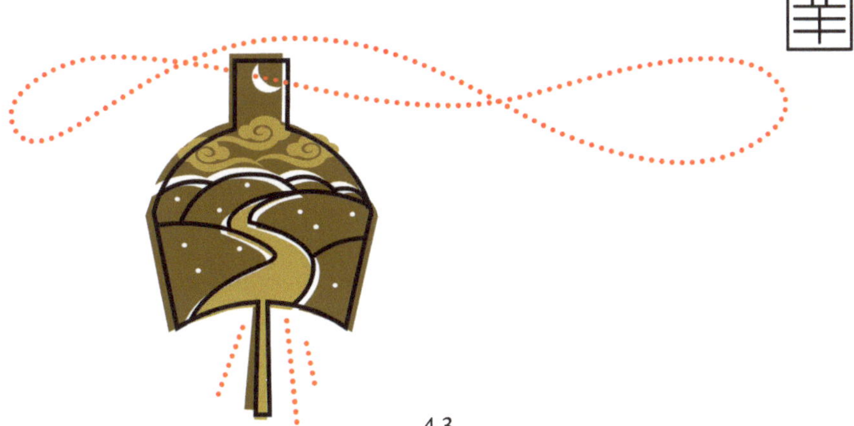

YEARS OF THE MONKEY
With auspicious monkey characteristics and other significant insights on page 88.

- 9 -

THE MONKEY

O F   T H E   S H A D O W L A N D   L A G O O N

The dragon (with the rabbit on its back) continued searching for the New Moon Circle, flying over the Misty Rolling Hills and beyond to the ocean. Holding tight to the dragon's antlers, the rabbit scanned the sea coast as the sun's final rays were fading into the shadow of darkness.

"I think I can just make out a circular lagoon below us," said the excited rabbit looking down, "and there's a round island at its precise center."

"Look, there's a great spherical banyan tree in the middle of that island. Could this be *the circle*? Let's fly closer," decided the dragon, diving down to the moon shaped island and alighting on the beach below the tree.

Suddenly, a series of boisterous screeches echoed from the branches above, sending confused birds and water fowl squawking for their lives and escaping into the sunset. The shouting seemed to be coming from an unhinged monkey swinging from vine to vine and creating a chaotic uproar.

45

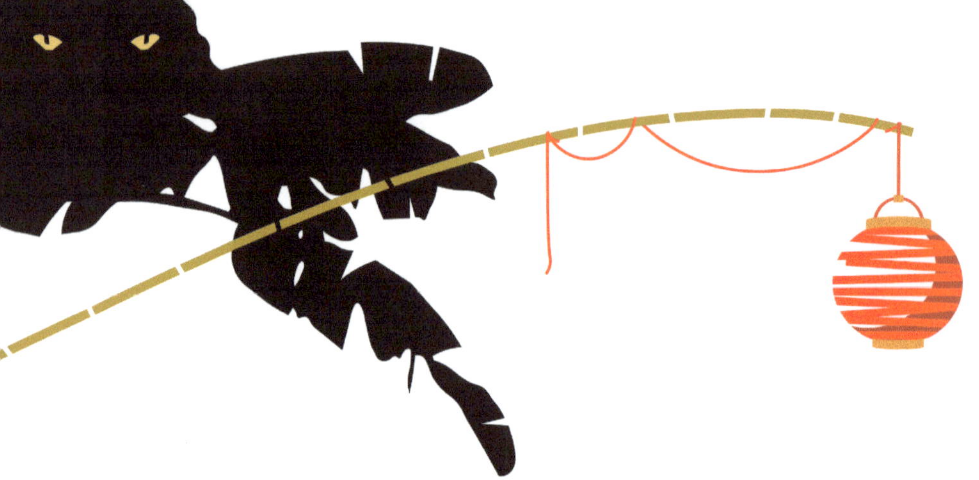

"Listen, Nian the Terrible, I'm telling you to leave Shadowland Lagoon AT ONCE!" cautioned the confident monkey, waving a rather dim and dysfunctional red lantern lashed to a long bamboo pole.

"Please calm yourself, monkey. I am NOT the monster, Nian. I am the dragon and this is the rabbit from the Emperor's Race twelve years ago. We mean you no harm. We landed on this island searching for the New Moon Circle."

Swinging on a vine, the monkey came closer to investigate the visitors and suddenly burst into loud laughter full of relief.

"Oh! He–he–he," giggled the suddenly cheerful monkey, "my mistake, I remember both of you. I am the monkey of the Shadowland Lagoon and you are most welcome here! I thought you were the beast that hates light," apologized the charismatic monkey swinging onto the beach. "Tonight, before the new moon, that horned monster, Nian, with the head of a lion and sharp teeth, will rise from the deep sea and destroy the crops and villages of this lagoon!"

"Excuse me, monkey, but why is your red lantern dark if Nian flees from bright lights?" inquired the rabbit sitting up high on the dragon's back.

"The lagoon's lanterns are torn and useless," explained the monkey, "so the flames do not last and go out quickly."

"What you need is my dragon fire—it burns continuously and never dims!" shouted the dragon.

"Oh, that's funny. I thought Chinese dragons brought rain and prosperity—not fire!" responded the confused, but good natured monkey, noticing smoke drifting from the dragon's nostrils.

"I have been exiled to this existence without those powers until I am deemed worthy. Until then, I am cursed with this furnace in my throat which I must control," the dragon responded somberly.

Jumping closer, the monkey cleverly smiled to himself, and then proposed, "If you will set a blaze in my red lantern and then light all the beacons throughout the lagoon before sunset, I will take you to someone special who I think can help you find the New Moon Circle. Agreed?"

"Agreed! But, who?—And where?" asked the dragon, lighting the red lantern.

"Why, at the Resplendent Village, of course!" chuckled the cheeky monkey, holding the glowing red lantern while climbing up the dragon's long tail.

Then, having lit all the lanterns of the Shadowland Lagoon and saved the villages from the monster Nian, the dragon that breathed fire (with the rabbit and now the monkey on its back) took flight for the Resplendent Village.

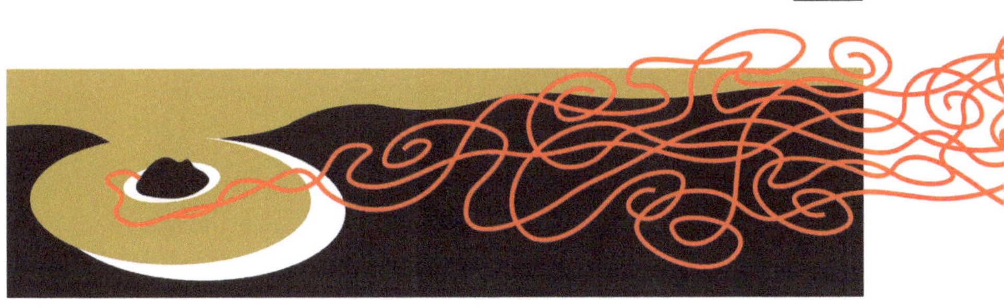

YEARS OF THE ROOSTER
With auspicious rooster characteristics and other significant insights on page 89.

- 10 -

THE ROOSTER
OF THE SUNDIAL PAGODA

The caravan of five travelers (with a cart half filled with rolled banners, scrolls, and couplets) wearily plodded towards the Resplendent Village. At the apex of another hill, a panorama of a fertile valley lay at their feet. Rows of orange and kumquat trees radiated out like spokes of an enormous wheel, and at the hub was a seven story pagoda tower. It stood in the sun's late afternoon light like an enormous sundial casting its long wavy shadow over the orchard.

"Being tethered to this wagon is challenging my spirit of independence," grumbled the restless horse with each lengthy mile.

"For two days now we've been progressing at a snails pace," complained the impatient tiger at the sheep's plodding gait. "Can we quicken our pace just a little?" asked the tiger, banging its own backside with the gong out of pure boredom.

"*It does not matter how slowly you go, as long as you do not stop,*" voiced the rat reading an ancient proverb on a scroll the ram selected from the cart. Continuing, the rat read, "*However, resting is like 'going' and necessary for strength. The rooster of the Sundial Pagoda is expecting us.*"

Moving through the circular orchards, they arrived at the tower, but the rooster was nowhere to be seen or heard. Bewildered, the rat, cat, tiger, horse, and sheep settled down at the pagoda's base and fell victim to slumber, sleeping deeply until…

"MORNING! THE SUN'S UP! THERE'S SO MUCH TO DOODLE-DO!" crowed the rooster from the tower's peaked rooftop. "I AM THE CROWNED HEAD OF MULTI-TASKING," babbled the boisterous rooster while popping into a window just below the top pyramidal roof. Using its large plumed tail feathers, the rooster began cleaning like a whirlwind, descending down the levels of the tower while squawking, "I DUST THE TOWER'S RAFTERS WHILE I SCOUR THE TOWER'S STAIRCASES! I MOP THE TOWER'S FLOORS WHILE I WIPE THE TOWER'S WINDOWS, RAILINGS AND PILLARS! I SWEEP AWAY THE BAD LUCK OF THE OLD YEAR, PREPARING FOR THE NEW YEAR!"

After cleaning the pagoda, the rattling rooster addressed the bleary-eyed animals by pointing to the orchard and with a vexatious volume shrieked, "THESE ORANGES AND KUMQUATS WON'T PICK THEMSELVES!"

"Whoa! Hold on," said the horse, stomping its right hoof. "We don't have time for this! Our destination, on this day, is the market at the Resplendent Village."

"BUT, DON'T YOU SEE?" shrieked the hysterical rooster, "THAT'S WHY YOU STOPPED HERE! I MUST GET MY CITRUS TO MARKET, DOODLE-TOO!"

"The rooster is correct," interjected the rat. "It says here on the sheep's scroll, and I quote: *A cart half full, must be filled with something. The golden fruit of the Sundial Pagoda brings good fortune. You may find what you seek by following the shadow path.*"

"How about THIS scenario," interrupted the cat to the rooster. "We agree to 'doodle-do' anything you ask, as long as you STOP YOUR LOUD CHATTING!"

"I DOODLE—do agree," said the regretful rooster, slowly speaking softly and with its wing pantomimed zipping up its beak.

Then, with a booming GONG from the tiger's mallet, two hefty baskets were pushed by the ram's horns to the half empty cart and then lifted into place by the tiger. The horse pulled the wagon into the orchard beneath the trees, as the rat climbed onto the branches and gnawed the stem of each orange and kumquat. The falling fruit was caught by the cat and rooster who tossed them into the baskets.

And with their backs to the rising sun, together the growing company of animals followed the direction of the Sundial Pagoda's shadow, hoping it would point them to the Resplendent Village and beyond to the New Moon Circle... in time.

YEARS OF THE DOG
With auspicious dog characteristics and other significant insights on page 90.

-11-

THE DOG

OF THE RESPLENDENT VILLAGE

The day before the eve of the Lunar New Year, the Resplendent Village was bustling with merchants and shoppers filling every shop beneath a vast canopy of freshly lit red lanterns. The dragon (with the rabbit and monkey on its back) had been sharing dragon fire by lighting every lantern throughout the land and was now resting in the courtyard on the steps of the Ancestor Hall. At the opposite end of the courtyard, having distributed the banners, scrolls, couplets, oranges, and kumquats at the market, the caravan of animals were gifting their earnings at a shrine. They burned red joss stick incense in beautiful brass pots honoring the memory of departed ancestors.

An air of excitement swept through the township and fluttered the rows of lanterns that were strung up for the lantern festival. Suddenly, excited barking swept into the center of the courtyard as the dog of the Resplendent Village jumped and danced about playfully.

Then, the silent ram began ringing its bell to pull focus.

"Gather around friends," said the monkey, moving to the middle. "This dog is wise, reliable and knows all that happens in this village. If the New Moon Circle is around here, this beloved dog will know."

The expanded group of animals stepped closer, forming a circle around the monkey and sheep, as the carefree dog in the center perked its ears, noticing all of them for the first time.

"Excuse us, kind hearted dog," said the rat, stepping forward. "We are the animals from the Emperor's Race and in need of your help. We have reason to believe that you may know the location of the New Moon Circle, which we seek. Our long quest has led us to you on the day before the eve of the Lunar New Year. All twelve of us must, by invitation, gather for a reunion at this circle by tomorrow night. Do you have any idea where the circle may be?"

"Maybe—but first, welcome, my friends. We have all drifted apart," responded the distracted dog. "Let's see—I count only eight of you—with me, that is nine. So, where are the ox, snake, and boar? Oh, wait—the boar."

Then, with a lengthy pause and deep in thought, the dog continued slowly trying to remember. "The boar lives hours from here in a craggy canyon—and is caretaker for a group of very tall timbers known as the Stately Grove. I've heard—there are old legends—about twelve gigantic trees that have been growing—in a perfect..."

"Circle," whispered the dog and the animals together.

Silence settled over the courtyard as the animals looked at one another and dared not speak.

Suddenly, total pandemonium broke loose as all the animals screamed as the tiger GONGED, the rabbit threw coins in the air, the sheep clanged its bell, and the rooster crowed YIPPEE-DOODLE-DO!

"By Jove, dog, you've done it," shouted the horse, standing up on hind legs. "You have found the New Moon Circle at long last!"

Turning to the gathered animals, the horse said, "Now, get some rest because we travel tonight and arrive at the Stately Grove at dawn!"

As the animals cheered and thanked the dog, the horse pulled the dragon aside and asked, "The ox and snake are at the Sheltering Stone Spa in the desert below the Tall Smokey Mountain. I promised I would return for them when the circle was found, but time is short. Would you please fly them to the Stately Grove when we arrive tomorrow morning on the Lunar New Year Eve?"

"It would be my honor," agreed the dragon, bowing its head.

"But, not without us," insisted the rabbit and monkey as they laughed and climbed onto the dragon's back. "Besides, you will get lost without my adorable fluffy white tail and this old red lantern!"

And so, the dragon (with the rabbit and monkey on its back) flew off together towards the Sheltering Stones Spa, while the remaining animals prepared for their night journey through a craggy canyon to the Stately Grove... and finally, to The New Moon Circle!

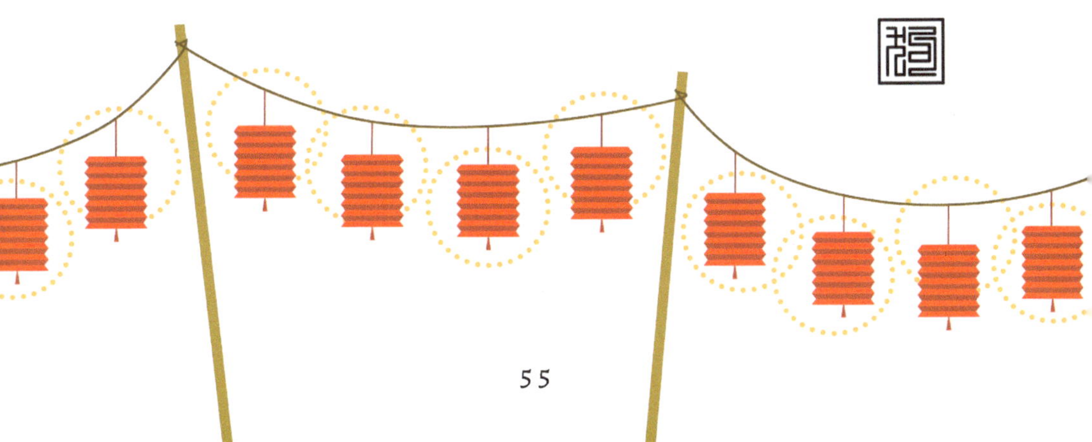

YEARS OF THE BOAR
With auspicious boar characteristics and other significant insights on page 91.

- 1 2 -
THE BOAR
OF THE STATELY GROVE

The soft colors of dawn could be seen on the horizon as the dragon (with the rabbit and monkey on its back, and now, the ox and snake hanging comfortably in a net clasped by the dragon's strong talons) spotted the bright lanterns of the parading animals below in a craggy canyon. After landing, the animals organized themselves in the order they had finished the race twelve years earlier, with the rat at the head of the line and the dog bringing up the rear.

"Well, I think we are getting closer to the Stately Grove—maybe," said the distracted dog while pawing the ground and chasing a chirping cricket.

"Shouldn't the dog be up front directing this trek?" asked the tired rat to the other animals while holding a small lantern which cast very little light.

In response, the voiceless sheep held up another scroll, and with a groan the rat unrolled the parchment and read: "It is written by the old master: *To lead a group, walk behind them.* And—*A good traveler has no fixed plans and is not intent on arriving.*"

"DAWN-a-Doodle-do!" crowed the rooster, interrupting the rat and making the animals jump.

"Quiet! Do you hear something?" whispered the tiger, stopping suddenly. "I hear weeping and gut wrenching wailing," said the rabbit. "Now, blubbering and bawling," bellowed the ox. "Ssssniveling. Ssssobbing," stated the snake. "That endless whimpering is coming from that clearing up ahead," announced the horse. "Let's explore," proposed the tiger, creeping through the underbrush.

Walking into an open area of the forest, the animals continued to hear the muffled crying, which seemed to be coming from under a heaping pile of sawdust and wood chips. Digging quickly, the animals freed the sorrowful soul and discovered the boar of the Stately Grove clutching a large bag of gold coins.

"Thank you and apologies for this dreadful state you find me in," sniffed the boar. "I am ruptured with sadness, and can do nothing but shed tears into what remains of this magnificent stand of mighty white pine trees. Look behind you at the ring of stumps that surround this clearing. Lumber was made of these grand pines twelve full moons hence and were carried away. I am the twelfth generation of boars that have been the caretakers of this grove. These pines were planted 144 years ago by the Jade Emperor himself only to be toppled, and in their place was left this red sack of gold coins."

In the dull glow of the dawn's light, the animals realized this was not the New Moon Circle that they had hoped for. Surrounding them were the scattered remnants and brutal relics of some of nature's grandest creations. In silence, the sorrowful animals turned and found a stump to sit on and began counting the rings of each tree's life.

"Err, excuse me," interrupted the cat, moving into the center, "I can see you are all sad as the reality of this devastating end to this quest becomes clear. In light of this turn of events, I'm moved to make a confession. There is no New Moon Circle. I made it up. I sent an invitation to the rat as a kind of joke at first, but as I thought about it, I became angry. I realized that after twelve years, I couldn't let go of how I was treated at the race and I wanted revenge. Not once, did any of you apologize to me. I was hurt and left to die (in some versions). So, now you know what it feels like to want something and have it torn away from you."

After a pause, the somber cat resumed, "However, seeing all of you like this makes me wish I had not deceived you. I forgive you all, especially you, rat."

There was silence and no one moved.

The Stately Grove was no more.

THE WAY

OF THE NEW MOON CIRCLE

Sadly the animals began to stir as if leaving to return to their separate homes, when a flickering ray of morning light danced on a young pine sapling. The animals turned, hearing the dog yelping and digging at the small pine tree's roots. The dragon looked on, pushing the dog aside and with its great clawed talons pulled the tree's root ball free from the soil. Something was glowing between its roots as the soil fell to the earth, and the dragon was left holding a large pearl.

Holding the glowing pearl up to the sky, the dragon began to spiral above the group, rotating in a circle. Instantly, the dragon's fiery breath was extinguished by water with a hot sizzle.

"It appears a higher power has deemed me worthy and I have been transformed once again into a rain deity," declared the dragon, soaring higher into the five-colored clouds above the animals.

"My course of action is now clear," announced the dragon with a thundering voice. "We will plant new white pine trees between the felled stumps and return the boar's progeny of caretakers to this Stately Grove."

"Lord Dragon-doodle-do," began the rooster without shouting, "I have skills with circular tree planting from years of tending to my fruit orchards. It would please me to organize and conduct the restoration of this grove back to its former glory."

"Granted!" declared the descending dragon, encouraging all the animals to follow the rooster's instructions, *tout de suite!*

With awe and growing enthusiasm the animals began to work together. The tiger scouted the area for new young saplings that were extracted by the dragon's talons and were carried next to each stump on the ox's back. Holes were dug by the dog and boar, then after planting, the soil was pounded firmly by the rabbit's feet. From the old forest floor, the ram's horns cleaved dried fallen trees into stakes that the horse dragged to the grove. Chomping the mallet, the tiger pounded the stakes beside each new tree. The monkey climbed up into the forest canopy looking for vines that the snake twisted into twine. The rat tied the twine from the stakes to the young pine's trunks, as the rooster pecked bugs off the new leaves, and then using its tail feathers swept the clearing free from sawdust and wood chips. Completed, the dragon rose up, admiring the fledgling grove circle, and conjured a heavy rain cloud that poured water onto each young new tree.

As the animals rested, the sheep walked to the center of the circle and spoke for the first time. With a quivering voice the ram said, "These are the words of the wise old master: *New beginnings are often disguised as painful endings. And, great acts are made up of small deeds.*"

"Thank you, profound ram," said the dragon stepping forward and speaking for the group, and then continued to address the animals. "The New Moon Circle does not exist. BUT, IF the circle *did* exist, I know where it is," said the dragon. "You see, the New Moon Circle is not a specific place but a pathway of many places. When the rabbit, monkey and myself returned to the Sheltering Stones Spa last night to collect the ox and snake, we traveled a loop over all the places you call home. The rabbit, as my navigator, pointed out that each of your homes were a day's journey by foot from each other. If a map were drawn of this route, it would be a great circle."

"Over the past twelve days as we followed the waning moon, we have come to realize that all things have a cycle and must be in motion," continued the dragon. "What has been revealed to all of us is that we have always lived in a circle—the New Moon Circle."

The animals began to stand up and move closer to hear the dragon's words. "However, now we need to complete the circle by helping this life energy flow, through what we now call the *Way of the New Moon Circle.* Our task is to close the gap and complete this cycle before the Lunar New Year."

"It's midday and I'm certain if we leave now we can arrive by midnight at my Blossoming Plum Tree where our journey began," projected the rat.

"Are we agreed, my dear friends?" roared the tiger with a GONG!

Through the shouts of agreement, the boar came forward and said to the animals, "Thank you. My ancestors appreciate what you have done this day." And then speaking for the animals, the humbled boar spoke to the cat. "We wish to apologize for our behavior at the Emperor's Race. We treated you poorly and are sorry for the years you have suffered. As restitution, I give you this red sack of gold coins. Now, dear feline, what do we call you?"

"Why, I'm the Fortune Cat of the Moon Gate Garden," purred the smiling cat, licking its paw.

THE CAT
With auspicious cat characteristics and other significant insights on page 92.

– 1 3 –

THE FORTUNE CAT
OF THE MOON GATE GARDEN

Turning back time to one month earlier, the cat slurped down the last noodle from a red bowl and then curled up for a nap on the Jade Emperor's lap.

"The movement of energy through the land is blocked," began the troubled Emperor from his palace, "and with the bridge almost finished, I'm hoping the cycle of life will finally flow with no end or beginning. However, I fear the twelve zodiac animals have something to do with this stoppage. They have become isolated, judgmental and even more competitive since the race twelve years ago. They've even ceased trying to improve themselves by not traveling or learning new things. Something has to be done."

"Who cares," yawned the cat, stretching its paws forward. "They get what they deserve. All they need is to confront each other and clear the air."

Deep in thought, the seated Emperor pushed aside a magnificent painted screen and gazed over the palace grounds. Far to the left stood the moon gate, plum tree and the garden beyond.

"I understand how unfairly the twelve animals treated you at the race," said the Emperor, stroking the cat's black fur, "and for this reason I have decided to bestow upon you the number: *Lucky 13*, with the title: *The Fortune Cat of the Moon Gate Garden*. However, you must earn this title. You say the animals can work out their differences by coming together? Find a way to make that happen by midnight on the eve of the Lunar New Year and the title is yours. Agreed?"

The cat had agreed to the Emperor's terms and now, one month later, the scheme had played out pretty well indeed. All that was needed was to get the animals through the craggy canyon, wide valley and across the river to the palace's Blossoming Plum Tree of the Moon Gate Garden in time. What could go wrong?

As the sun was setting, the snake was traveling comfortably in a basket woven by the rat and hanging from the Pan Chang knot around the ox's neck. The animals were helping each other along the trail when the rabbit started hopping in a circle and looking around.

"I'm having a very serious *déjà vu* right now," said the confused rabbit. "If I'm n-not mistaken, we have been here before."

"Yes—I do believe you're right," said the dog, catching up with the others.

"This is the Emperor's race course from twelve years ago," exclaimed the animals in unison, stopping in their tracks dreading another crossing of that tempestuous and perilous water.

"That means the river is over the next hill," stated the dragon, flying up to get a better look.

"I say—*Once more unto the breach, dear friends, once more...*" quoted the golden stallion, preparing for an arduous swim.

"My resilient travelers," declared the dragon, hovering high above the group of blocked animals, "it appears that a bridge has been built for us. Quickly now—you all must see this remarkable structure."

Winded, the animals stood on the rushing river's bank and discovered a beautiful crimson arched bridge, built of twelve tall wood pillars, six on each side of the path. On the top of these strong columns sat gold gleaming carved sculptures of themselves—the twelve zodiac animals.

At the entrance to the bridge was a brass plaque that read:

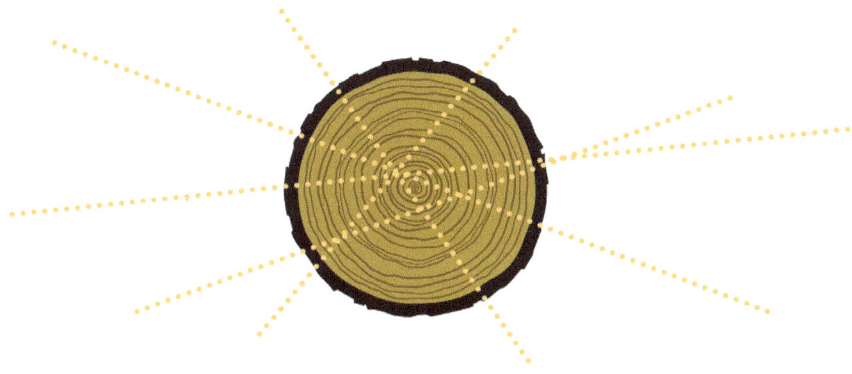

THE BRIDGE OF THE MIGHTY WHITE PINES
IN HONOR OF THE WHITE PINE TREES OF THE STATELY GROVE
THAT WERE USED IN THE CONSTRUCTION OF THIS BRIDGE, AND
IN TRIBUTE TO THE TWELVE ZODIAC ANIMALS WHO TOGETHER
OPENED THE "WAY OF THE NEW MOON CIRCLE."

Your path is made for a journey, not a destination.

Then, through the sunset's last rays of light, the cat crossed the Emperor's arched bridge first, stopping at the crown, turned and raised its paw, beckoning the animals to follow.

- 1 4 -

AN EPILOGUE

THE NEW YEAR PANDA

All thirteen animals crossed the bridge onto the palace grounds by dark and made their way to the Blossoming Plum Tree of the Moon Gate Garden. Together, holding lanterns and laughing as a group, the zodiac animals forgot about the order they had won the race twelve years earlier. Their quest had been fulfilled and the cycle completed a few hours before midnight.

Outside the moon gate, the rat climbed up through the familiar branches of the old plum tree as the last of late winter's petals fell onto the cat, who stood below looking up.

"Friends again?" asked the cat, as the rat sat on top of the moon gate looking at the faint ghost of the new moon.

"Look, cat—I'm sorry for everything, I…" began the rat.

"Now, you know better" interrupted the cat, "and so—you'll do better. Besides, we have our rival reputations to uphold. Our friendship will be our little secret."

After a pause, the cat licked its paw and asked, "Agreed?"

"Agreed," said the smiling rat.

"So—tell me cat, you've been the Jade Emperor's lap pet all these years? And just when I thought you were such a tough street feline. What does he call you?" teased the rat, scurrying over the moon gate.

"Lucky 13," shouted the cat, chasing after the rat to join the others.

Then suddenly, the garden came alive with the sound of the tiger's GONG! GONG! GONG!, as the animals celebrated the Lunar New Year… together.

Every year the twelve (or rather, thirteen) zodiac animals would travel the same path as they did on that twelfth year, crossing the river and completing the cycle that flowed energy through the Way of the New Moon Circle. Sharing support and using their own unique set of skills, talents and experience these friends felt the power of the circle at work in all their lives.

THE PANDA
With auspicious panda characteristics and other significant insights on page 93.

Without exception, on each Lunar New Year Eve, they would arrive at the Moon Gate Garden with more friends, gifts, food, traditions and eventually the celebration would last many more days.

A new host emerged, the New Year Panda, whose role became important in Chinese culture as a symbol of friendship and peace. Each new year the Jade Emperor arranged for *Pixiu* (which is the ancient name for 'panda') to preside over the festivities. Known as the "sacred creature of the forest," the panda would travel down from the Min Shan Mountains to reside in a bamboo forest that the emperor had planted on the palace grounds. In return, the panda's mere presence would ward off evil spirits and protect the Way of the New Moon Circle from natural disasters.

Like clockwork on the Lunar New Year, fireworks and firecrackers would light up the sky chasing away bad luck and over time, the terrifying stories of the monster, Nian faded from memory—while below in quiet temples, joss sticks burned in smoky vessels in remembrance of beloved ancestors.

Under the glittering stars and through a craggy canyon, the thriving white pine saplings of the Stately Grove grew a few inches each year—as festivals and colorful parades filled the streets of the Resplendent Village and then over-flowed into neighboring towns.

The Sundial Pagoda's tower remained spotless, as its orchards expanded to include tangerines and pomelos... and a hen house.

The villages of the Shadowland Lagoon began producing the finest and most sturdy red lanterns in all the land—as artists, ceramicists, sculptors and calligraphers flocked to the Misty Rolling Hills.

The wind of the Boundless Plain became a perfect place for kite flying and the training ground for racing—as the Sheltering Stone Spa remained a sanctuary for tranquility and health (because some things should not change too much).

The Tall Smoky Mountain was transformed to the Mountain of the Floating Fluffy White Clouds where waterfalls cascaded from every cliff and a shrine was built in a high cave to honor past ancestors.

On the grasslands of Whatever Comes Next, stargazers came with telescopes to study the cycles of planets—and as fear diminished in the Deep Deep Jungle, new music, instruments and dances were developed to dazzle and entertain.

And finally, the Distant Meadow evolved into the Meditation Meadow, a place for inner growth and manifesting desires. All this transformation was supported by an anonymous source that legends say involved a red sack filled with gold coins that never seemed to diminish and was simply called "Lucky 13."

So, the story continues, with each Lunar New Year when fire-works explode over *the circle* and the rain dragon (with the rabbit and monkey on its back) appears in the night sky bringing protection and prosperity to the land.

"By the way, cat, how *did* you end up at the Jade Emperor's palace?" asked the rat years later, after traveling the circle a few times.

"Originally the gods appointed 'yours truly' to run the world; however, I couldn't be bothered, so I proposed humans for the job instead," explained the cat licking its paw.

"Then," continued the cat, "having all the time in the world to nap (like cats do), *and* after surviving the Great Race, the Emperor saw me laying about and gave me this gig."

"Is that so..." replied the distracted rat, while observing the beauty of the night sky above them.

Then, like old pals sitting side by side on the moon gate, the rat and the cat silently watched the evolving moon as it made its slow journey toward the horizon—and then disappeared.

- 15 -

AFTERWORD

THE CIRCLE OF ANIMALS

MEANING AND MYTHOLOGY IN
CHINESE AND ASIAN CULTURE WITH
AUSPICIOUS ANIMAL CHARACTERISTICS
AND OTHER SIGNIFICANT INSIGHTS

THE CIRCLE OF ANIMALS CHART, page 79

1- YEARS OF THE RAT, page 80

2- YEARS OF THE OX, page 81

3- YEARS OF THE TIGER, page 82

4- YEARS OF THE RABBIT, page 83

5- YEARS OF THE DRAGON, page 84

6- YEARS OF THE SNAKE, page 85

7- YEARS OF THE HORSE, page 86

8- YEARS OF THE SHEEP, page 87

9- YEARS OF THE MONKEY, page 88

10- YEARS OF THE ROOSTER, page 89

11- YEARS OF THE DOG, page 90

12- YEARS OF THE BOAR, page 91

13- THE CAT, page 92

14- THE PANDA, page 93

QUOTES, listings and credits, pages 94, 95

AUTHOR'S NOTE, page 96

THE CHINESE ZODIAC IS AN ANIMAL ROTATION in an established order that's repeated every 12 years and is used to denote the year of a person's birth. Each lunar year, the new moon begins this cycle explaining why the term *zodiac* is translated in western astrology as the 'circle of animals'.

WHAT THE EMPEROR'S RACE REVEALS is that the twelve animals of the original legend are created with human emotions, strengths and weaknesses. Over time, each of these animals began to form specific personalities and relationships with each other. Chinese astrology is now a complex rotating multiple chart system of these zodiac animal signs that calculates how people perceive or present themselves to others and themselves.

THE RAT

MEANING AND MYTHOLOGY IN
CHINESE AND ASIAN CULTURE WITH
AUSPICIOUS RAT CHARACTERISTICS
AND OTHER SIGNIFICANT INSIGHTS

Wisdom

*The Rat's energy is YANG and considered
active, hot, aggressive, masculine and light.*

*The Rat's fixed element is WATER, which
features the traits of being sympathetic,
a perfectionist and an ideal coordinator.*

YEARS OF THE RAT: 1912, 1924, 1936, 1948, 1960, 1972, 1984, 1996, 2008, 2020, 2032, 2044

THE RAT represents wisdom and is the first in the twelve-year cycle of zodiac animals. Known for their keen sense of adaptability, rats are quick-witted, resourceful, and smart but lack courage. With rich imaginations and sharp observation skills, they can take advantage of various opportunities. Rats are likely to be alert, cheerful, popular, intelligent, practical, charming and ambitious— but if not careful they can be timid, stubborn, talkative, greedy, devious, and eager for power.

PLUM BLOSSOMS mark the end of winter and the return of spring. Since they are considered the first flower of the new year, they represent renewal. The plum blossom, known as *the meihua* in Chinese, symbolizes hope, courage, strength, resilience and perseverance in the face of adversity, thriving in contrary circumstances by budding in winter's chill. The Plum Blossom was officially designated the national flower of China on July 21, 1964.

A MOON GATE is a circular pedestrian passage through a wall into a Chinese garden and is considered a source of luck or good fortune for those who step through it. Rising visually up out of the landscape, a moon gate is symbolic of birth and renewal. The birth of a new moon is the way in which time is marked and the new comes about.

THE OX

MEANING AND MYTHOLOGY IN CHINESE AND ASIAN CULTURE WITH AUSPICIOUS OX CHARACTERISTICS AND OTHER SIGNIFICANT INSIGHTS

Diligence

The Ox's energy is YIN and considered passive, cool, relaxed, feminine and dark.

The Ox's fixed element is EARTH which features the traits of being kind, tolerant, honest and a great leader.

YEARS OF THE OX: 1913, 1925, 1937, 1949, 1961, 1973, 1985, 1997, 2009, 2021, 2033, 2045

THE OX represents diligence and is the second in the twelve-year cycle of zodiac animals. Known for being hardworking, oxes are likely to be exceptionally clever and creative. The ox hates to fail at anything, thus being very successful in life and willing to make great sacrifices for the ones they love. Known for handling things steadily, oxes are trustworthy, honest, ambitious, cautious, gentle and loyal—but if not careful they can be quick tempered, stubborn and known for not being great communicators.

CHINESE KNOTS are traditionally created to express good wishes, including happiness, prosperity, love and the absence of evil. These knots are used today as good luck charms to decorate homes during festivals and celebrations. The beautiful *Pan Chang* knot communicates a belief in a cycle of life with no beginning and no end.

QIGONG MEDITATION is an ancient Chinese healing practice that combines meditation, relaxation, controlled breathing and gentle movement to maintain balance. *Qigong* (pronounced "chee-gong") is roughly translated as 'the master of one's energy.' This practice is meant to cultivate the energy and strength found in nature into one's body to promote better mental, physical, and spiritual health.

THE TIGER

MEANING AND MYTHOLOGY IN
CHINESE AND ASIAN CULTURE WITH
AUSPICIOUS TIGER CHARACTERISTICS
AND OTHER SIGNIFICANT INSIGHTS

Bravery

The Tiger's energy is YANG and considered active, hot, aggressive, masculine and light.

The Tiger's fixed element is WOOD which features the traits of being exceptionally gifted, idealistic and a good planner.

YEARS OF THE TIGER: 1914, 1926, 1938, 1950, 1962, 1974, 1986, 1998, 2010, 2022, 2034, 2046

THE TIGER represents bravery and is the third in the twelve-year cycle of zodiac animals. Tigers are natural born leaders and display overwhelming generosity to those close to them. Known for their great confidence, tigers can be competitive, fearless, powerful and courageous risk takers living life to the fullest. Tigers are both friendly and charming—but on the flip side they can be impetuous, irritable, overindulged and love to boast to others.

CHINESE GONGS date back 5500 years as a symbol of spiritual power and protection. Used in ceremonies to announce persons of authority, gongs served as a status symbol of wealth. In rites, the Gong was used in the evocation of ghosts with memories of the past. In East Asian cultures it is thought that touching a gong can bring you good fortune, strength and happiness.

PERCUSSION INSTRUMENTS are used for many purposes in Chinese culture including lavish ceremonies, festivals, weddings, solemn commemorations and for wartime marches. Throughout Chinese history, drums and bells were often used to tell time. The Chinese drum, the *tanggu* is a red ceremonial drum used for theatrical performances and rituals, whose rhythms are based on and symbolize the heartbeat.

THE RABBIT

MEANING AND MYTHOLOGY IN
CHINESE AND ASIAN CULTURE WITH
AUSPICIOUS RABBIT CHARACTERISTICS
AND OTHER SIGNIFICANT INSIGHTS

Longevity & Luck

The Rabbit's energy is YIN and considered passive, cool, relaxed, feminine and dark.

The Rabbit's fixed element is WOOD which features the traits of being exceptionally gifted, idealistic and a good planner.

YEARS OF THE RABBIT: 1915, 1927, 1939, 1951, 1963, 1975, 1987, 1999, 2011, 2023, 2035, 2047

THE RABBIT represents longevity & luck and is the fourth in the twelve-year cycle of zodiac animals. Known for being kind-hearted, rabbits are honest with a high degree of integrity as well as being discreet, diplomatic and well respected. They are meticulous about their appearance and prefer a calm, secure and stable environment. Rabbits can be friendly, intelligent, cautious, skillful, and gentle. They dislike fighting and find solutions through compromise—but if not careful, have the potential to be superficial, stubborn and melancholy.

RED PACKETS are monetary enveloped gifts, most commonly used during the Lunar New Year as a symbol of good fortune and prosperity, and to ward off evil spirits. The red color is considered a symbol of luck, life and happiness in Chinese and other East Asian cultures. The legends associated with the origins of the red envelopes vary, but most include an evil entity that was defeated.

THE MOON FESTIVAL is an evening celebration where families gather together to light lanterns, eat moon cakes and appreciate the full moon which is a symbol for family reunion. Celebrated in the mid-autumn, this harvest festival is held on the 15th day of the 8th month of the Chinese lunisolar calendar with a full moon at night. The rabbit, in Chinese culture is known as a symbol of selflessness and because of that was rewarded by the moon goddess, *Chang'e* to live with her on the moon. It is said, if you look up at the moon on a clear night you can see the markings of the rabbit on its surface.

THE DRAGON

MEANING AND MYTHOLOGY IN CHINESE AND ASIAN CULTURE WITH AUSPICIOUS DRAGON CHARACTERISTICS AND OTHER SIGNIFICANT INSIGHTS

Prosperity

The Dragon's energy is YANG and considered active, hot, aggressive, masculine and light.

The Dragon's fixed element is EARTH which features the traits of being kind, tolerant, honest and a great leader.

YEARS OF THE DRAGON: 1916, 1928, 1940, 1952, 1964, 1976, 1988, 2000, 2012, 2024, 2036, 2048

THE DRAGON is known as the symbol of China and represents prosperity. Dragons occupy the 5th position in the twelve-year cycle of zodiac animals. As the only supernatural being in the zodiac, the flying dragon is known for bringing good luck. They love to travel, often searching for the most exotic destinations. Dragons are known for being powerful, kind-hearted, successful, innovative, brave, and courageous—but if not careful, can be conceited, tactless, quick-tempered and over-confident.

THE GLOWING PEARL being chased by a dragon is a common image found in Chinese art and folklore. The pearl, (known also as the flaming pearl) when possessed by the dragon as a rain deity, is a symbol of wisdom, spiritual energy, power, protection and longevity.

CHINESE DRAGONS are mythical benevolent creatures and are different from western dragons physically. Chinese dragons fly without wings and are composed of various animal parts such as the body of a snake, head of a camel, mouth of an alligator, antlers of a deer, ears of an ox and tail of a fish. The red dragon is the strongest symbol for good luck and prosperity in China.

THE CLOUD motif in Chinese art and culture is perceived as a symbol of Heaven, and the five-colored auspicious clouds as a Kingdom at peace. *Yun*, the word for 'cloud' sounds like the Chinese word for good fortune. "Clouds soar up to end in rain," is a poem used to teach Chinese characters to children since the sixth century.

THE SNAKE

MEANING AND MYTHOLOGY IN CHINESE AND ASIAN CULTURE WITH AUSPICIOUS SNAKE CHARACTERISTICS AND OTHER SIGNIFICANT INSIGHTS

Transformation

The Snake's energy is YIN and considered passive, cool, relaxed, feminine and dark.

The Snake's fixed element is FIRE which features the traits of being courageous, passionate and a quality researcher.

YEARS OF THE SNAKE 1917, 1929, 1941, 1953, 1965, 1977, 1989, 2001, 2013, 2025, 2037, 2049

THE SNAKE represents transformation and is the sixth in the twelve-year cycle of zodiac animals. Snakes are usually calm observers with excellent intuition, and generally demonstrate intelligence, wisdom, and creativity. Known for being wise and mysterious, snakes prefer a calm and placid life and can be introverted which is often misunderstood as secretive and elusive. Snakes can be discreet, agile, attractive and full of sympathy— but if not careful, there is a tendency for them to be lazy, greedy, arrogant and indulging in self-admiration.

THE GOURD or calabash plant (known as the *Wulu*) is a symbol of good health, longevity and prosperity in Chinese culture and is an important tool used in enhancing the effects of *feng shui*. As a charm to ward off disease and evil spirits, the gourd can also be used as a bottle, a dipper or a musical instrument.

YIN & YANG is deeply rooted in Chinese beliefs and represents duality of all things in the universe, or the idea that two opposite characteristics can actually exist in harmony and complement each other. Yin and yang is a Chinese philosophical concept that describes opposite but interconnected and synergistic forces.

FENG SHUI is an ancient Chinese art of arranging buildings, objects, and space in an environment to achieve harmony and balance. This practice is a belief that the way your house is designed and the way that you arrange objects affects your success, health, and happiness. *Feng shui* means 'the way of wind and water.'

THE HORSE

MEANING AND MYTHOLOGY IN
CHINESE AND ASIAN CULTURE WITH
AUSPICIOUS HORSE CHARACTERISTICS
AND OTHER SIGNIFICANT INSIGHTS

Independence

The Horse's energy is YANG and considered active, hot, aggressive, masculine and light.

The Horse's fixed element is FIRE which features the traits of being courageous, passionate and a quality researcher.

YEARS OF THE HORSE: 1918, 1930, 1942, 1954, 1966, 1978, 1990, 2002, 2014, 2026, 2038, 2050

THE HORSE represents independence and is the seventh in the twelve-year cycle of zodiac animals. Horses have a free, passionate spirit and are in their element outside enjoying physical activities. As tireless workers, horses are always moving toward a goal, but need variety and challenges in their lives. They can survive any obstacle by being quick thinking, clever and intuitive. Known to be friendly, generous and popular, horses have the ability to persuade others—but if not careful they can be selfish, arrogant and over-confident.

A FAN in China is a symbol of protection and wealth. Fans move good chi that filters bad chi, thus harnessing the flow of lucky life energies. Originating in China, **KITES** (known as a carrier of hope) were constructed like fans, with bamboo and silk. On the *Qingming* (means 'clearness' or 'brightness') Festival, people fly kites as far as possible and then cut the line, allowing the kites to drift with the wind. This is a symbol of letting go of the unhappiness and sadness accumulated in the previous year.

BAMBOO WIND CHIMES can be traced back to ancient China and were created for practical purposes like signaling changes in weather or approaching danger. These chimes hold significance in Chinese culture as they harmonize spaces by welcoming abundance and attracting positivity while dispelling negative energies.

NUMBER EIGHT

THE SHEEP

MEANING AND MYTHOLOGY IN CHINESE AND ASIAN CULTURE WITH AUSPICIOUS SHEEP CHARACTERISTICS AND OTHER SIGNIFICANT INSIGHTS

Creativity & Calmness

The Sheep's energy is YIN and considered passive, cool, relaxed, feminine and dark.

The Sheep's fixed element is EARTH which features the traits of being kind, tolerant, honest and a great leader.

YEARS OF THE SHEEP: 1919, 1931, 1943, 1955, 1967, 1979, 1991, 2003, 2015, 2027, 2039, 2051

THE SHEEP represents creativity & calmness and is the eighth in the twelve-year cycle of zodiac animals. Known for being peaceful and gentle outside but tough inside, the sheep has a strong sense of solidarity, harmony and imagination. Rams favor a tension free environment and a love of nature and wildlife. Known to get along with everyone, the sheep is a team player, kind-hearted, sincere and compassionate—but if not careful they can sometimes be pessimistic, unrealistic and slow in their behavior.

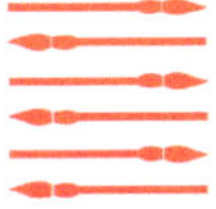

CALLIGRAPHY is the art of brushwork and ink, that reveals the secrets of heaven through written characters. In China, calligraphy is considered not just a form of decorative art, but viewed as a supreme visual art form of self-expression and cultivation. The custom of writing spring couplets for the lunar new year, consists of pairs of verses that are written in black or gold ink on red paper with symbols representing wealth, health, protection and good luck. These banners are traditionally hung on walls and around doorways or windows to express good wishes for the coming year.

HANGING METAL BELLS are hung from eaves at the entrances to temples and pagodas in China to ward off evil spirits and communicate with ancestral spirits. Richly decorated and cast in bronze, these hanging bells (as per *feng shui*) are highly auspicious and safeguard your home from bad luck. In a Chinese meadow, a moving flock of sheep will follow a ram that wears a neck bell.

THE MONKEY

MEANING AND MYTHOLOGY IN CHINESE AND ASIAN CULTURE WITH AUSPICIOUS MONKEY CHARACTERISTICS AND OTHER SIGNIFICANT INSIGHTS

Flexibility

The Monkeys energy is YANG and considered active, hot, aggressive, masculine and light.

The Monkey's fixed element is METAL which features the traits of being determined, persistent, a workaholic and an expert manager.

YEARS OF THE MONKEY: 1920, 1932, 1944, 1956, 1968, 1980, 1992, 2004, 2016, 2028, 2040, 2052

THE MONKEY represents flexibility and is the ninth in the twelve-year cycle of zodiac animals. Known for being cheerful, high-spirited and energetic by nature, monkeys are extremely self-confident and as a result may become mischievous when bored. They are efficient decision makers with good common sense and are known for being intelligent, clever, innovative and shrewd. Monkeys can be charming, loyal, and charismatic—but if not careful they can become jealous, arrogant and egotistical.

RED PAPER LANTERNS are symbols of wealth, fame, and prosperity and are hung at Chinese celebrations. Lanterns symbolize letting go of the past year and welcoming the new year with good fortune. The color red, seen throughout Asia during the lunar new year, is considered good luck and represents life, vitality, and light. Also, red banners and lanterns with tassels are used to decorate doorways to ward against evil spirits and bad luck.

NIAN THE TERRIBLE, according to a Chinese legend, was a terrifying demon-monster and a hideous beast with sharp teeth and sharp horns that was believed to appear on new years eve to destroy crops, animals and terrorize people. Because Nian feared the color red, loud noises and fire, red paper lanterns were burned all night, and firecrackers were lit to frighten the monster away.

THE ROOSTER

MEANING AND MYTHOLOGY IN CHINESE AND ASIAN CULTURE WITH AUSPICIOUS ROOSTER CHARACTERISTICS AND OTHER SIGNIFICANT INSIGHTS

Fidelity & Punctuality

The Rooster's energy is YIN and considered passive, cool, relaxed, feminine and dark.

The Rooster's fixed element is METAL which features the traits of being determined, persistent, a workaholic and an expert manager.

YEARS OF THE ROOSTER: 1921, 1933, 1945, 1957, 1969, 1981, 1993, 2005, 2017, 2029, 2041, 2053

THE ROOSTER represents fidelity & punctuality and is the tenth in the twelve-year cycle of zodiac animals. Roosters are methodical, well organize and achievement oriented wanting the best of everything. Known for being talkative, outspoken and frank, roosters like to keep things neat and organized. Though they thrive in formal settings, roosters yearn for attention and excitement. Also, Roosters can be hard-working, courageous, independent, humorous and honest—but if not careful they can sometimes be arrogant and self-aggrandizing.

THE ORANGE is the food symbol of the Chinese New Year bringing good luck and happiness. Oranges, with their round shape and glowing hue reminiscent of gold, symbolize money in traditional Chinese customs. The color *orange* in Chinese resembles the word for 'luck & wealth', while *gold* (as the sun) symbolizes 'prosperity'. On the first day of Chinese New Year, families and businesses roll oranges and coins over the threshold of their front door, to ensure that prosperity will flow into the building all year long.

CLEANING is traditional for families in China before the start of the new year. Tidying up the house by getting rid of dirt, rubbish and unwanted items is symbolic of driving away the bad luck of the previous year for a fresh new start. The word *dust* in Chinese is a homophone for 'old', thus cleaning the house is symbolic of sweeping away all the negative energy from the old year and welcoming in positive energy for the new year.

THE DOG

MEANING AND MYTHOLOGY IN
IN CHINESE AND ASIAN CULTURE WITH
AUSPICIOUS DOG CHARACTERISTICS
AND OTHER SIGNIFICANT INSIGHTS

Loyalty & Honesty

The Dog's energy is YANG and considered active, hot, aggressive, masculine and light.

The Dog's fixed element is EARTH which features the traits of being kind, tolerant, honest and a great leader.

YEARS OF THE DOG: 1922, 1934, 1946, 1958, 1970, 1982, 1994, 2006, 2018, 2030, 2042, 2054

THE DOG represents loyalty & honesty and is the eleventh in the twelve-year cycle of zodiac animals. Known for being dependable, dogs are not materialistic and find happiness helping others and worthy causes. Though more comfortable in smaller groups, dogs are friendly and have a good sense of humor. Dogs are known for being smart, devoted, kind, reasonable, true, faithful, straight forward and have a strong sense of responsibility—but if not careful they can be stubborn, critical of others and awkward in certain social situations

THE LANTERN FESTIVAL celebrates the first bright full moon of the year and marks the departure of winter and the beginning of spring. Fifteen days after the shadowy new moon, the lanterns symbolize driving out darkness to bring hope in the coming year.

JOSS STICKS are a type of incense that is made up of various herbs and burned at Chinese New Year as a way of paying respect to ancestors and warding off bad luck. The scent of the joss stick is believed to calm the human spirit and improve health. Traditionally, the passing of time was also measured by the burning of a set length of this type of incense.

SHOPPING before the New Year celebration is centered around welcoming the new and the good after removing the bad and the old. Marketplaces are filled with shoppers buying decorations and traditional dishes such as dumplings, fish, sweet rice balls and oranges that are all considered lucky for the new year.

THE BOAR

MEANING AND MYTHOLOGY IN
CHINESE AND ASIAN CULTURE WITH
WITH AUSPICIOUS BOAR CHARACTERISTICS
AND OTHER SIGNIFICANT INSIGHTS

Wealth & Luck

The Boar's energy is YIN and considered passive, cool, relaxed, feminine and dark.

The Boar's fixed element is WATER, which features the traits of being sympathetic, a perfectionist and an ideal coordinator.

YEARS OF THE BOAR: 1923, 1935, 1947, 1959, 1971, 1983, 1995, 2007, 2019, 2031, 2043, 2055

THE BOAR represents wealth & luck and is the twelfth in the twelve-year cycle of zodiac animals. Boars are hard workers, realistic, lucky and blessed with good fortune. They are intelligent, courageous and fight for what is right. Known for being kind-hearted, understanding and patient, boars can be shy and difficult to know. They may appear to be gullible and innocent, but their simplicity should not be mistaken for weakness. Boars are known for being generous, docile and easygoing—but if not careful they can become self-indulgent, clumsy and lazy.

GOLD COINS represent prosperity in China and are integral to Lunar New Year celebrations symbolizing abundance and good fortune. Gifting gold items, such as coins and jewelry, is customary to wish wealth and prosperity for the year ahead. *Feng shui* coins with carved holes and images, are lucky to attract wealth and can increase their power by being hung together with red cords.

WHITE PINE TREES can survive in harsh conditions and are a symbol of long life in Chinese culture. Commonly used in art and literature, the white pine symbolizes longevity, tenacity and nobleness because they are evergreen. Slow growing, these pines can take over 200 years to reach 100 feet in height, growing six inches a year.

THE CAT

MEANING AND MYTHOLOGY IN CHINESE AND ASIAN CULTURE WITH AUSPICIOUS CAT CHARACTERISTICS AND OTHER SIGNIFICANT INSIGHTS

Good Fortune

In ancient China, people thought Cats were mystical creatures with amazing spiritual powers. Even today, if you keep a Cat well fed and safe, it is believed they will frighten away evil spirits and bring wealth and luck to your home.

THE CAT in ancient China, was kept by both the rich and poor, but was the beloved companion for the nobility and thus found its way into poetry and art. In Chinese mythology, the gods initially put cats in charge of the world after they created it. However, the goddess Li Shou, who was the leader of the cats, noticed that these felines had other ideas and wanted only to laze about in the sun. So, Li Shou suggested that humans seemed to be more interested in running things and that cats would rather just enjoy the world.

THE BECKONING CAT welcomes customers as a symbol of good fortune for small business owners throughout Asia and now the world. According to a folktale, the poor owner of a shop took in a starving stray cat despite barely having enough to feed himself. In gratitude, the cat sat in the front of the store beckoning customers, thus bringing prosperity as a reward to the charitable proprietor. From then on, the "beckoning cat" or "waving cat" has been a symbol of good luck. In fact, throughout Chinese history, even black cats were considered a powerful force for good rather than bad luck as in the western world.

LONGEVITY NOODLES or *yi mein*, are served at Chinese New Year celebrations to signify a long life and good luck. This custom of eating longevity noodles at celebrations has been passed down for generations. The two foot long strands are to be eaten whole without breaking. The longer these noodles remain intact, the longer your lifespan—maybe even "nine lives" for you, your cat and loved ones.

THE NUMBER THIRTEEN is a lucky number in China, which translates to 'assured growth' or 'definitely vibrant'. Known as unlucky throughout the western world, the number 13 according to *feng shui* in Chinese culture, sounds like the word for a long life.

NUMBER FOURTEEN

THE PANDA

MEANING AND MYTHOLOGY IN CHINESE AND ASIAN CULTURE WITH AUSPICIOUS PANDA CHARACTERISTICS AND OTHER SIGNIFICANT INSIGHTS

Friendship & Peace

The Panda's energy is YIN & YANG and is considered the embodiment of both. Which is why the highly prized and gentle Pandas of ancient China graced the gardens of the emperors and were believed to have incredible mystical powers.

THE PANDA has an important role in Chinese culture as a symbol of friendship and peace and is a spirit animal that brings both gentleness and power. The panda's black and white coloring is considered a physical depiction of *yin & yang* and its balance brings about harmony and tranquility. This duality is continued in the written character for panda which is both the bear and the cat. Good humor and tenderness are the terms most often associated with pandas.

THE GIANT PANDA was seen as a symbol of strength and bravery and used by emperors for protection and even healing. In ancient times the panda was called *Pixiu* and was a symbol of both peace and strength. Even today pandas were given as gifts from China to other countries as a symbol of peace and friendship.

THE MYTHOLOGY of how the panda got its black markings is considered an old Chinese folklore tale. It was said that originally pandas were all white. One day a shepherdess was out with her sheep when she saw a panda being attacked by a leopard. She grabbed a stick and attacked the leopard, which allowed the panda to escape from its jaws. Unfortunately the leopard killed the girl instead. At that time, it was a mourning ritual to rub black ashes on the body. Many pandas came to the funeral out of respect for the shepherdess. While they wiped tears from their eyes and hugged each other for comfort, they smudged the black ashes into each other's fur.

FIREWORKS are traditionally set off on New Years Eve to scare away evil spirits creating a safe and healthy new year. Around 200 BC, the Chinese unintentionally invented firecrackers by tossing bamboo into fire, but it took another thousand years before true fireworks exploded in the night sky. It is believed that a cook accidentally invented gunpowder by mixing three common kitchen ingredients.

QUOTES

LISTINGS AND CREDITS

LAO TZU (c. 6th century BC) was an ancient Chinese philosopher whose name is sometimes spelled Laozi. As the founder of philosophical Taoism, Lao Tzu is author of the *Tao Te Ching* that roughly translates as 'the way of integrity.' Its verses describe how to live in the world with goodness and honor. While most of his life remains a mystery, Lao Tzu's writings and main beliefs emphasize simplicity, humility and harmony with the natural world. As a title of respect in China, Lao Tzu is typically translated as "the Old Master."

A journey of a thousand miles begins with a single step.
—LAO TZU, front cover & page 14

If you do not change direction,
you may end up where you are heading.
—LAO TZU, page 25

To a mind that is still the whole universe surrenders.
—LAO TZU, page 26

With no desire, at rest and still,
All things go right as of their will.
—LAO TZU, page 39

To lead a group (people), walk behind them.
—LAO TZU, page 57

A good traveler has no fixed plans and is
not intent on arriving.
—LAO TZU, page 57

New beginnings are often disguised as painful endings.
—LAO TZU, page 62

Great acts are made up of small deeds.
—LAO TZU, page 62

RALPH WALDO EMERSON (1803-1812) was known as the "Sage of Concord" and one of the greatest philosophers that the United States ever produced. As an American essayist, lecturer, abolitionist and poet, Emerson inspired a new way of thinking and was an advocate of social reforms. Some of his most well-known essays are *Self-Reliance*, *The Over-Soul*, *Experience*, *Circles*, *The Poet* and *Nature*.

It's not the destination, it's the journey.

—RALPH WALDO EMERSON, pages 1, 43 & 67
(Paraphrased by the Sheep:
Your path is made for a journey, not a destination.)

CONFUCIUS (551-479 BC) was a contemporary of Lao Tzu and was also a philosopher and seeker of spiritual truth. Perhaps one of the most well known Chinese sages, he was the founder of Confucianism. His writings dealt with a wide variety of subjects including ethics, politics, the pursuit of knowledge and was the first teacher in China to advocate for mass education.

*It does not matter how slowly you go,
as long as you do not stop.*

—CONFUCIUS, page 49

WILLIAM SHAKESPEARE (1564-1616) was an English playwright, poet and actor. He is widely regarded as the greatest writer in the English language and the world's pre-eminent dramatist. He wrote 154 sonnets and 38 plays and is often called England's National Poet and the "Bard of Avon." Not only did Shakespeare teach us about ourselves and humanity, but he also invented around 1700 words which are still used in everyday English today.

Once more unto the breach, dear friends, once more...

—WILLIAM SHAKESPEARE, page 66
(From the play: *King Henry The Fifth*, Act III, Scene I)

AUTHOR'S NOTE

This allegory of a meaningful journey is a work of fiction and from my imagination. While this short novel was inspired by the myth of the Chinese Jade Emperor's Great Race, the creation of these anthropomorphic characters and their relationships have been born out of Chinese culture both ancient and modern. I have tried to respectfully honor the traditions, legends, philosophies, culture, art, writings and history of China through my own lens to serve this story. However, this is in no way a complete guide to Chinese new year celebrations or zodiac horoscope information. My use of "old master" is inclusive of many wise philosophical works from the writings of Lao Tzu and Confucius and some may be a paraphrased translation in the language and dialog of the characters of this story. The ram rehashes the words of Ralph Waldo Emerson and there's also a Shakespeare-quoting horse that makes this point. Often, these playful animals speak with a contemporary flair and use language of a more modern humor such as the cat's snarky quips.

In writing this story's allegorical narrative, the themes of forgiveness, diversity, getting unstuck and facing fears (among others) have been assigned to the animals of this adventure. Ultimately these characters become united while passing through diverse lands, customs, ancestry and extended households, and friendships are born out of differences—regardless of their many variances. As each animal travels their own personal journey of discovery, it's the giving, sharing and circulating of their unique characteristics that makes them stronger together as a group in reaching their quest.

As the dragon simply said to the rabbit, "—together, we'll go further."

What drew me to write and illustrate this book is the beautiful use of symbolism and meaning in the natural world of the Chinese culture and philosophy. It speaks to me and I have loved sharing this journey with you.

The end of one path is the beginning of another...